Duncan's
New Friend

For Jack

First published in Great Britain under the title of Duncan and the Bird
in Picture Lions in 1992
This edition published in 1999
1 3 5 7 9 10 8 6 4 2
ISBN: 0 00 664710 3
Picture Lions is an imprint of the Children's Division,
part of HarperCollins Publishers Ltd.
Text and illustrations copyright © A Vesey 1992

Printed and bound in Singapore by Imago

Duncan's
New Friend

Amanda Vesey

Picture Lions
An Imprint of HarperCollins*Publishers*

High up in a tree Duncan had a house.

He never felt lonely in his tree house; he liked messing about there all by himself.

One morning when Duncan went to his tree house he had a surprise. On his bed, nestling in the blankets, was an egg.
It was a very large egg.

Duncan looked up large eggs
in his bird book.

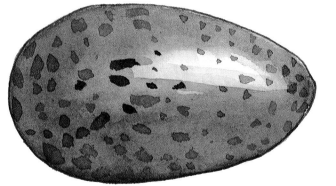

It wasn't the egg of an
Arctic Loon.

Or a Bennets Cassowary.

Or a King Penguin.

The egg in Duncan's tree house wasn't in the least like
any of the large eggs in the bird book.

Duncan picked up the egg and shook it. Something inside the egg moved. Something inside the egg squawked.

Duncan placed the egg carefully back in the blankets and watched it.

He watched it all afternoon until suppertime, but nothing happened.

Next morning Duncan could hardly wait to get back to his tree house. He ran up the ladder and through the front door.

The egg was gone.

His bed was all messy and crumpled and when he looked closer he found large pieces of cracked eggshell in the blankets. There was more eggshell on the floor.

"Squawk!" said something behind him.

Sitting on the floor, behind the door, was a large baby bird. A bird with a green and yellow beak, black spikey feathers and red, webbed feet.

"Hullo!" said Duncan, "what kind of bird are you?"

Duncan went back to the bird book.
   The bird wasn't a toco toucan –
they have coloured beaks but
the wrong sort of feet.

It wasn't a tufted puffin –
they have webbed feet but
a different kind of beak.

   It wasn't a horn bill or a pelican or a crane or a
blue-faced booby.
   The bird in Duncan's tree house wasn't like any
of the birds in the bird book.

"Where did you come from?" asked Duncan. He bent down to pat the bird's head, to show he was friendly.

Do you know what some birds do if you get too close? They peck you.

This bird pecked Duncan. It had a large beak and it was a hard peck.

"You must be hungry," said Duncan. "I had better find you some food."

"Worms," thought Duncan. "Worms are what baby birds like to eat." He dug about in the vegetable patch until he found one. Then he carried it back to the bird.

"Here's a nice juicy worm," said Duncan.
"Open your beak and I'll pop it in."
   The bird inspected the worm.
   Then it stared at Duncan.
   Its beak stayed firmly shut.

"Caterpillars," thought Duncan.
"Baby birds like to eat big fat hairy caterpillars."

He found a nice green one, munching a leaf.

The bird had its beak open, and was
making a hungry cheeping noise.
Duncan dangled the caterpillar
over its open beak.

"Look, Bird," said Duncan.
"A lovely green crunchy
caterpillar. Eat it up."
     The bird eyed the caterpillar.
Then it gazed at Duncan.

Its beak shut with a snap.

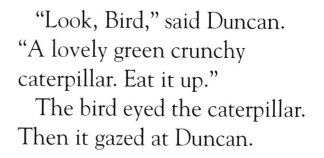

"You are a silly bird," said Duncan. "If you won't eat worms, and you won't eat caterpillars, what will you eat?"
The bird gave Duncan a look. A look that said: would *you* eat worms and caterpillars?

"I'll have to try something else," said Duncan.

Duncan went home and raided the larder. He put a tin of baked beans, some cold fish fingers left over from the day before, a pot of peanut butter and a piece of chocolate cake into a carrier bag.

He took them back to the tree house.

"Baked beans?" offered Duncan. "Fish fingers? Peanut butter? It's delicious on toast."

The beak stayed firmly shut, but the bird stared hard at the chocolate cake.

"Cake!" said Duncan. "Let's try that." The beak began to open very wide.

Duncan popped the cake into the bird's beak, and it disappeared at once. Not a crumb was left.

"That's what you like," said Duncan. "You're a cake-eating bird. I'll have to fetch more cake!"

Duncan spent all his pocket money on slightly stale cakes which he got half price from the bakery.

The bird grew and grew. It took up the whole of the camp bed, and lay there most of the day, reading comics and waiting for the next meal.

Duncan liked the bird, but sometimes he wanted his tree house to himself. Was this bird never going to fly?

"It's time you learnt to fly," said Duncan. He pushed the bird to the top of the ladder.

"Jump!" said Duncan.

The bird peered at the ground far below, then it stared at Duncan. Its feet stayed firmly on the ladder.

"Shut your eyes," said Duncan, "and try jumping off a bit lower down."

The bird had several goes from the lower rungs of the ladder. Each time it landed with a thump on its flat webbed feet.

It became very hot and cross.

"Try again from the top," ordered Duncan. "And this time flap your wings hard as you jump."

The bird jumped. It flapped.
Then just as Duncan thought
there was bound to be a crash landing,
the bird soared up into the air.
"You can fly!" called Duncan as the bird
flew over the tree tops and out of sight.

Over the river and round the village flew
the bird. Over the church tower and the petrol
station and the school playground. Over the
new bungalows and the rubbish tip and the big
house – what was this?
The people at the big house were having a
grand garden party. A wonderful tea was spread
out on long tables under a cedar tree.

"Oh, joy!" thought the bird, swooping down to the table. There were little cakes with pink icing and cherries on the top. There was chocolate fudge cake and upside down cake and walnut cake and Black Forest gateau.

Gulp! The bird swallowed a whole walnut cake. Snap!
A plateful of fairy cakes vanished down its throat. Munch!
Crunch! Champ! Chomp! Jellies wobbled off their plates,
milk jugs flew, cups and saucers twirled and spun.

   The tea party broke up in total disarray.

"Mercy! Fetch the Fire Brigade!" cried the Mayor fainting into the arms of the vicar's wife.

"By Jove, that's a rum-looking bird," barked the Colonel. "I wish I had my gun."

"Whatever has happened?" gasped Duncan. He was late for the party because his mother had made him change his clothes.

"A gigantic bird flew down and ate all the cake," they told him. "It was as big as an albatross and black as a raven. You've never seen anything like it!"

Duncan thought he had.

"Anyone at home?" called Duncan, when he got back to the tree house.

There was no sign of the bird. On the table, melting slightly, was a wonderful ice-cream cake, topped with strawberries and meringues.

Somewhere, far above the trees, Duncan heard a distant, self-satisfied squawk.